This book belongs to:

....

....

Retold by Monica Hughes
Illustrated by Gwyneth Williamson

Reading consultants: Betty Root and Monica Hughes

This edition published by Parragon in 2009

Parragon
Queen Street House
4 Queen Street
Bath BA1 1HE, UK

ISBN 978-1-4075-8369-3

Printed in China

Cinderella

Bath · New York · Singapore · Hong Kong · Cologne · Delhi · Melbourne

Helping your child to read

These books are closely linked to recognized learning strategies. Their vocabulary has been carefully selected from the word lists recommended by educational experts.

Read the story
Read the story
to your child
a few times.

When Cinderella got to the ball she saw the prince.
Cinderella fell in love with the prince.
The prince fell in love with Cinderella.
They danced all night long.

20

Follow your finger
Run your finger under
the text as you read.
Your child will soon begin to
follow the words with you.

Look at the pictures
Talk about the pictures. They will
help your child to understand the story.

The prince fell in love with Cinderella. *21*

Give it a try
Let your child
try reading the
large type on each
right-hand page.
It repeats a line
from the story.

Join in
When your child is ready, encourage
him or her to join in with the main
story text. Shared reading is the first
step to reading alone.

Once upon a time there was a beautiful girl called Cinderella.
Cinderella had two ugly sisters.
The ugly sisters were unkind to Cinderella.

Cinderella had two ugly sisters.

One day Cinderella and her sisters got
an invitation.
It was from the prince.
It was an invitation to a ball.
The ugly sisters said to Cinderella,
"You can't go to the ball!"

"You can't go to the ball!"

The ugly sisters said to Cinderella,
"You don't have a ball dress.
You don't have a coach."
The ugly sisters put on their
ball dresses.
Then they got into their coach and
went to the ball.
Cinderella was very sad and she began
to cry.

Cinderella was very sad.

Then Cinderella's fairy godmother
came to see her.
"Don't cry, Cinderella," she said.
"You can go to the ball."
But Cinderella said, "I can't go to
the ball.
I don't have a ball dress and
I don't have a coach."

"You can go to the ball."

The fairy godmother waved her wand.
Now Cinderella had a beautiful coach.
The fairy godmother waved her
wand again.

The fairy godmother waved her wand.

And Cinderella had a beautiful ball
dress and some little shoes.
"Now I can go to the ball," she said.
"But you must come home by
midnight," said her fairy godmother.

Then Cinderella got into her
coach and went to the ball.

"Come home by midnight."

When Cinderella got to the ball she
saw the prince.
Cinderella fell in love with the prince.
The prince fell in love with Cinderella.
They danced all night long.

The prince fell in love with Cinderella.

Then Cinderella saw the clock.
It said midnight.
"I must be home by midnight," said
Cinderella.
So Cinderella ran away from
the prince.
As Cinderella ran away she
lost one little shoe.

Cinderella ran away.

The prince picked up the little shoe.
"I love the girl who fits this little
shoe," he said.
Every girl wanted the little shoe to fit.
The ugly sisters wanted the little
shoe to fit.
But the little shoe did not fit.
Then Cinderella put on the little shoe.

Cinderella put on the little shoe.

And the little shoe did fit Cinderella.
The prince was happy and
Cinderella was happy.
Cinderella and the prince were
happy ever after.

Cinderella and the prince
were happy ever after.

Look back in your book.
Can you read these words?

sisters

Cinderella

coach

wand

fairy godmother

Can you answer these questions?

Who sends an invitation
to a ball?

Why is Cinderella sad?

What does Cinderella
lose when she runs
away from the ball?